THE FOXES OF CHIRONUPP ISLAND

Story and pictures by

HIROYUKI TAKAHASHI

English translation by

ANN KING HERRING

Windmill Books, Inc.
and E. P. Dutton & Co., Inc.
New York

First published in the U.S.A. 1976 by Windmill Books and E. P. Dutton | First published in Japan 1975 by Kinnohoshi-Sha | Text and illustrations copyright © 1975 by Hiroyuki Takahashi | English translation copyright © 1976 by Windmill Books and E. P. Dutton | All rights reserved | Library of Congress Cataloging in Publication Data | Takahashi, Hiroyuki. The Foxes of Chironupp Island. | Translation of Chironupp no kitsune. | SUMMARY: The old couple who visits the small island every summer befriends a tiny fox cub. The lives of all of them change dramatically in the ensuing years when war comes to Japan. | [1. Foxes—Fiction] I. Title PZ7.T143Fo | [E] 76-9033 ISBN: 0-525-61544-X | Printed in Japan by Dai Nippon | 10 9 8 7 6 5 4 3 2 1 | Designed by The Etheredges

Just off the northern tip of Japan, a small island rises
out of the cold seas. It is called Chironupp.

In the spring of each year, the same old couple returned
to the island—always at the same season, when the fox-roses
began to bloom.

This is the story of what happened on the island one year,
not long before the great war between men began.

The winter snow ceased falling. The great ice floes in
the surrounding seas broke up and began to drift away.

In a cave in the heart of the birch forest that covered
the island, two little foxes were born.
The elder of the two was a dog fox cub, a male.
The younger cub was a vixen, a female.

When the two little foxes were weaned, their parents taught

them to recognize different sorts of prey by smell.

Unless they learned to do this, they would not be able to

fend for themselves when they grew up.

Every day, the father fox brought home the game he had caught

and hid it in the bushes. Then he called the cubs.

The fox cub always came running.

But the vixen cub showed little interest.

She preferred chasing butterflies.

At the top of a hill on the island was a small stone statue of Jizo, the patron saint of children and of life.

The statue was in the form of a little girl. No one could say who had carved it and how long it had stood there.

Here and there at the foot of the statue, the small white blossoms of the fox-roses were coming into bloom.

The old couple folded their hands in prayer to the little stone saint.

"This year, too, we've come back to the island for our summer work. Help us to live safely and happily and to bring in a good catch of fish."

"Why, look! What a dear little fox cub!"

Perhaps the cub had somehow become separated from her
parents and lost her way, for she trotted after the old couple,
following them all the way to their cottage at the foot
of the hill.

The old woman brought out some small fish, and the cub
ate them quickly.

When she saw that the little fox showed no signs
of returning to the forest, the old woman tied a red ribbon
around the vixen's neck. Then she tucked a fox-rose
into the bow.

"Now, then, you stay here with us and be our child,
until you've grown a little bigger. How would you like
that, Tiny?"

Tiny quickly found herself very much at home with
the old couple.

Sometimes she went walking on the island with the old woman,
who gathered cresses, coltsfoot, and other wild herbs.

On other days, she would go out in the fishing boat
with the old man.

Even in midsummer, the northern seas are cold.

Day after day, heavy mists hang over the water, and the sun

seldom shows its face.

One afternoon near the end of summer, the old woman

was busy working on the shore, drying the strands of seaweed

she had gathered.

Tiny was just as busy playing.

Suddenly, a dark shadow loomed up through the mist.

"Anything new on the island?"

The shout came from a patrol boat manned by soldiers
who were guarding the northern seas.

"Look there! A fox!"

One soldier raised his gun.

Holding Tiny tightly, the old woman turned and
tried to run away, but she tripped and fell.

Fortunately, however, the soldiers did not try to land,
and they soon sailed off.

When the birch groves on the island began to turn to gold,

it was time for the old couple to leave for the winter.

The old woman took Tiny and went to the little stone statue

of Jizo to say farewell.

"We are thankful for all of the fish we have caught.

Tomorrow morning, we must leave your island once again."

She looked at Tiny for a long time, while the fox cub

nestled in her arms. Then, as though her mind was made up,

she put Tiny down and retied the ribbon in a looser knot.

"Today you must go back to the place where your mother lived.

You will be happiest there. Good-bye, and good luck!"

From somewhere deep in the forest, they could hear

the far-away barking of a fox.

The next morning, the old people left the island.

The old man had to row hard, for the boat was full of fish

and dried seaweed and it rode low in the water.

"Look there, Mother! It's a whole family of foxes!"

"Why, so it is. And look. Our Tiny's with them."

The old woman leaned out over the gunwale of the boat

and shouted:

"Tiny! TINY! We'll be back to see you next year,

when the fox-roses bloom. Be waiting for us then!"

The four foxes soon resumed their everyday pattern of living.

On clear moonlit nights, they all gathered at the
top of Jizo Hill.

The male cub was very fond of mouse-hunting games.
Whenever the father fox brought a live mouse to him, he would
leap at the mouse and try to catch it.

The seasons changed and soon the cold north winds

whistled through the trees.

The little foxes grew and grew. Their heavy coats

were sleek and shining.

One day, the male cub went all alone down to the stream

that flowed near the foot of Jizo Hill. The salmon had come

back to these waters to lay their eggs, and he thought

he would try his hand at fishing.

Bang!

All at once, a strange, menacing noise split the air.
The fox cub suddenly fell over and lay still.
At the top of the hill, the father fox gave a loud bark
of warning, sprang up and began to run.

Bang! Bang! Bang!

The strange sounds rang out again. With a yelp of pain,
the mother vixen stumbled and fell. But in an instant
she was up again, and all three foxes were racing toward
the shelter of the trees.

It was dark and quiet in the shadow of the birch trees.

The father fox licked the vixen's leg wound and tried
to stop the pain.

One night passed by, and then another. The male cub
still did not return.

Tiny was hungry. She left her parents and wandered away,
searching here and there for something to eat.

"Ki-yi-yi-yi! Help! Help! Help!"

It was Tiny's voice.

The mother and father fox froze and listened intently.

They realized something was very wrong.

Then they ran off, speeding through the forest toward the spot

where the yelps of pain were loudest.

They found Tiny lying near a bamboo-grass thicket.

She kicked and struggled, but she could not run away, for an

iron snare bit into her leg and held her fast.

It was a trap that the soldiers had set and left there.

The father fox sniffed at the trap and pulled it,

but he could not free Tiny's leg from its jaws.

Tiny shrieked with pain.

The fox bit at the chain, but even his sharp teeth

were no match for the cruel steel.

The wind blew, bringing a smell of danger to their noses—
the smell of men and gunpowder. The soldiers
were coming closer.

The mother quickly gathered some leaves and twigs
and covered Tiny with them. Then she, too, hid in the
bamboo-grass thicket.

The father gave one sharp bark. He turned and began to run—
deliberately heading into the wind, where the scent of
danger was strongest.

Faintly but clearly, gunshots echoed from the foot of the hill.

The father fox did not come back.

Now, only the vixen remained. All she could do was go on
catching things to eat and bring them to Tiny.

Dragging her wounded leg behind her, she did her very best,
carrying food to Tiny day after day. The biting wind blew,
the rain came, and at last it turned to sleet.

The first snow had begun to fall.

The vixen's wound became more and more painful,

until she could hardly walk.

Now she hunted no longer. It was even difficult to

find berries and a few small insects to eat.

Soon the forest floor was covered with a white sheet of snow.

Tiny opened her eyes and gazed up.

The flakes of snow drifting down from the sky looked

like many starry petals from blooming fox-roses.

The vixen lay down in the snow and covered Tiny with
her warm, furry tail.

The warmth enveloped Tiny. She was no longer cold.
Overcome by drowsiness, forgetting her hunger, she soon fell
fast asleep.

The snow continued to fall, covering the mother and her cub
with a heavy white blanket.

In time, the snowfall ended.

The seas around the island froze over. Gigantic walruses lumbered out of the water to rest on the huge cakes of ice.

Months passed. Once more, heavy mists shrouded the island, and the ice began to break into smaller pieces and drift away.

Spring had come at last.

Snow-lilies, dandelions, violets, and choke-cherries all burst into flower.

Soon it was time for the fox-roses to bloom.

But this year, the old man and his wife did not come to the island, for now the country was at war.

Finally, the war came to an end. Several more springs came
and passed into summers.

One day, a small boat drew near and landed on the island.

The fisherman and his wife had come back at last.
They looked careworn and very old.

At the top of the hill, the fox-roses were blossoming
in a solid sheet of white.

The two old people stared at the flowers in wonder.

"I don't remember seeing so many of them blooming
like this before."

"St. Jizo, St. Jizo, here we are again—here we are at home."

"I wonder what happened to Tiny?"

The old couple walked through the meadow and into the
birch forests beyond.

There they found two mounds of fox-roses—one large,
the other one small. The shapes looked almost like
a mother fox and her cub.

Beside the smaller cluster of flowers, half-buried in
the grass, there lay an old chain covered with rust. And in
the midst of the white blooms, they saw a single bright
red flower. It looked to them like a ribbon tied in a bow.

The bright blue of the sky and the dark blue of the seas—

these alone remained unchanged from the years before.

For a long time, the old man and the old woman stood silently

at the top of the hill. They had no need of words

for their hearts were filled with memories.